PLEA

MW01282502

Justin Isis has worked as a model, consultant, rap-per and visual artist. His previous works include *I Wonder What Human Flesh Tastes Like* (Chômu Press, 2011), *Welcome to the Arms Race* (Chômu Press, 2015), and *Divorce Procedures for the Hairdressers of a Metallic and Inconstant Goddess* (Snuggly Books, 2016). He also edited Chômu's *Dadaoism* anthology (2012), *Marked to Die: A Tribute to Mark Samuels* (Snuggly Books, 2016) and *Drowning in Beauty: The Neo-Decadent Anthology* (Snuggly Books, 2018). He currently lives in Tokyo.

SNUGGLY BOOKS

JUSTIN ISIS

PLEASANT
TALES
II

THIS IS A SNUGGLY BOOK

Copyright © 2018 by Justin Isis.

All rights reserved.

ISBN: 978-1-943813-73-5

CONTENTS

PLEASANT TALES II

THE LAMBS IN THE TRENCHES
ARE LAMBENT AND TRENCHANT

Maja and Ebba liked to eat chocolate pudding.

The best kind came in packs of six, sealed with a plastic top. When Maja and Ebba went grocery shopping with their mother, they would take packs of the chocolate pudding from the shelves and place them in the grocery basket.

"No, that's too much," the mother sometimes said.

Other people in the aisle would turn and watch as the mother placed the chocolate pudding back on the shelf. Maja and Ebba became sad. They would run off when the mother was in a different aisle and take the chocolate pudding again. The pudding packs were usually frosty from the shelf, but when Maja and Ebba carried them, close to the chest, the frost disappeared and the packs became warmer.

Maja and Ebba didn't wait until they got home to eat the chocolate pudding. The packs came with plastic spoons and Maja and Ebba would tear them from the lids. They took a single pack each. The mother was left to carry the groceries.

Ebba walked head down, staring into the pudding. The chocolate surface spread through the pack's gently curving cylinder. Ebba took the lid flap between her thumb and forefinger.

Maja ran out and spun in circles. She stretched her arms and twirled across the parking lot. The mother watched her and carried the bags to the car.

Inside, Maja and Ebba opened the chocolate pudding. They pulled the flaps back slowly, stripping the plastic from the glue that sealed it to the lid. The packs croaked softly as they opened. A thin brown ring remained on the back of the flap and Ebba licked it off. Maja saved hers for later. She scooped out the pudding with her red plastic spoon. As she ate, she felt a sweetness at the back of her mouth.

The mother leaned around and said, "Don't eat too much."

When they arrived home the father came out. The father helped carry the bags inside. He tried to pat Maja and Ebba on the head and they made faces at him, smiling. The father saw the chocolate pudding smeared around the edges of their mouths. When Maja and Ebba finished, traces of pudding remained in the packs. Maja reached a finger in and scraped it off and sucked her finger.

At other times they would sit in the street, eating. The sun went down and they became silent.

The father watched their jawbones moving. First their mouths opened to accept the spoon. Then their jaws closed. Sometimes a cheek would puff out. Sometimes their tiny mouths opened and closed, slowly. The father had seen fish breathing that way.

The father looked out into the street as the sun went down.

He saw people crossing at the corner. A man

passed him wearing a shirt that said 'Punjab.' His daughters' mouths filled with pudding.

A tiny chain of lights opened in his mind. The father closed his eyes and the lights swirled in darkness. They gave off scattered grains, like pollen. The vast night of time opened before him. The father felt weightless.

The lights said, 'Punjab, Punjab, Punjab.' Gently, Punjab lifted itself out of space and floated behind his eyes. He could see it reflected upside down. A ripple passed across its surface, and the lights vanished. He had heard Punjab called "India's breadbasket state" before.

$$\Omega$$

Stevens shifted at the podium. Kuldeep Singh was twiddling his thumbs again. This peculiar habit of Mr. Singh, who always sat in the front row, had been a source of constant distraction throughout the semester.

"Farming of the kinnow, popularly called the stepbrother of the orange, has picked up considerably among farmers occupying some 5,000 hectares with an overall yield of 300,000 tonnes annually," Stevens said. But now it was impossible for him to concentrate, and he recited the rest of the lecture in a monotone, hardly hearing his own words.

He left Punjab Agriculture University at 3:30 and, after receiving a phone call, went to the post-office to pick up a package. Later, in his office, he opened it and found several photos of his family. In the first set, his nephews were playing in a garden, their feet covered in dirt.

He looked up as the bell rang. It was Amrik from his second-period class. Stevens motioned for him to come in.

"Here's my report," Amrik said, handing him a folder. "I'm sorry it's late. I needed to finish my research on crop rotation."

Stevens looked at him. He was carrying a grocery bag in his left hand. Through the plastic he could see the outline of a thick block of chocolate.

A tiny chain of lights opened in his mind. Stevens closed his eyes and the lights swirled in darkness. They gave off scattered grains, like pollen. The vast night of time opened before him. Stevens felt weightless.

The lights said, 'Chocolate pudding, chocolate pudding, chocolate pudding.' Gently, a plastic cup of chocolate pudding lifted itself out of space and floated behind his eyes. He could see it reflected upside down. A ripple passed across its surface, and the lights vanished. He had eaten chocolate pudding of this kind before.

♌

Both men returned home at 9:30 p.m. and watched television for an hour while eating dinner. An hour later, when they went to bed, both pulled back the corner of the sheet from the left and then stopped suddenly. It seemed that they had pulled back the sheet in the same way before, and that something of great importance attached itself to the motion. Remembering it implied remembering something else, and for a moment an endless series seemed to shimmer out of reach. Then they forgot it, climbed into bed and slept facing the left, both their knees bent at the same narrow angle.

A WALK IN THE PARK

Soon after his eighteenth birthday Gaurav Gupta decided to take specific, measurable, achievable, realistic and time-bound steps to improve himself. Until then he had been taking it easy on himself, disdaining physical activity and listening exclusively to classic emotional hardcore and even some legitimately obscure, mostly instrumental post-metalcore that both indulged and amplified his persistent feelings of self-pity. Gaurav concluded that this was not a productive long-term strategy that would bring him closer to personal fulfillment, but until now there had been no real impetus to embark on a journey of transformation.

The turning point was a life-changing encounter with Giancarlo, the best soccer player at Gaurav's high school in Butchers Hill, Maryland. Gaurav was cutting through Patterson Park on his way home from his monotonous and unremunerative job at the Carvel Ice Cream Shoppe when he noticed Giancarlo practicing wall juggling against the side of the public toilets. He was wearing a yellow Neymar Jr. jersey and a pair of black and yellow Adidas Nemeziz 17+ 360 Firm Ground Agility cleats. Giancarlo's facial expression conveyed a quiet, rapt, monastic, self-satisfied and yet unpretentious concentration.

"Gaurav how's life recently?" Giancarlo asked as Gaurav walked over to him.

"Not very good bro. I am usually lying down on my bed listening to Saetia and pg. 99, or else I am at Carvel selling various ice cream novelty items such as the 'Flying Saucer,' a circular ice cream sandwich; the 'Icy Wycy,' a paper cone of sherbet on a stick; the 'Brown Bonnet' and 'Cherry Bonnet,' frozen vanilla ice cream on sugar cones dipped in a sweet, waxy confection; the 'Tortoni,' a cup of vanilla ice cream covered with toasted coconut and topped with a maraschino cherry; and the 'Lollapalooza,' a cylindrical mound of ice cream on a stick covered with colored sprinkles. I am mostly just jerking it to PornHub facesitting videos and not going on any dates or anything."

"Doesn't sound like your current situation is very goal-oriented," Giancarlo admonished accurately.

"I can't seem to get anywhere with the interpersonal relationships with females, and I'm feeling a bit uncertain about the future," Gaurav complained exasperatedly. "I also feel that my motivations are fairly self-centered and I don't really have that much intrinsic compassion for people whose circumstances are radically different from my own, such as individuals of other genders and also the differently abled."

"That's because you don't have a clear sense of where the goal posts in your life are," Giancarlo said. "It's like you're just dribbling in place all the time. You need to work out a clear offensive strategy."

"Can these soccer metaphors be productively applied to other life goals bro?" Gaurav asked.

"Yes, in fact, these metaphors are firm yet flexible like the underside of these Adidas cleats I am wearing and can comfortably encase a number of other life situations in the same way the cleats encase my feet. For example, there is a lot of footwork involved in sales. Or legwork you might call it. You want to be careful not to put your foot in your mouth when working with long-form sales letters, and remember to use negative qualification too. Spike the defense when necessary, but always keep your eye on the goal, and don't let your enthusiasm get the best of you, which might result in a yellow card. Now let me ask how is your diet?"

"It's hell basic . . . just a lot of Subway sandwiches and Mountain Dew."

"Not really any way to manage your macros. Right now you can't see the goal posts because you don't have basic emotional and dietary ball control down. It might seem like a lot of balls to juggle but until you establish a serious diet and training routine, you won't even get to take a penalty kick when life fouls you out. Just remember that the future is going to keep moving the posts . . . but life's goalie isn't always paying attention."

Gaurav saw at once the truth of Giancarlo's words. His parents were prosperous doctors who had worked hard to provide for him, and it was now time to get over himself and begin taking concrete steps towards change. He resolved to stop listening to the emotional hardcore, or any other guitar-based music that conveyed depressive emotions, and begin improving his diet, exercise and outlook. He returned home at once and made a list of his goals:

FACIAL DYNAMICS—sharpen up
Finance skillz—investigate day trading and Forex
Overall gainZ—run tren soon?
Spiritual wholeness/wellness—need UNITY
Differently abled bros—pump compassion
Achieve quantum mindset

Over the next few years, Gaurav expanded on each point of his checklist. He learned about investment, and took a number of free online courses on SEO strategy. He joined mastermind groups on Facebook and zestfully subjected himself to lectures by Tony Robbins and Eric Thomas. After eleven months of more or less constant work he was able to attain complete financial independence through the success of his digital marketing projects. From there he paid a ghostwriter and several other content creators to put together a video course and webinar that would explain the methods he himself had taken to attain wealth, with a focus on proper mindset and motivation. He expanded his investment portfolio and hired several college students to develop more original content for him, which he marketed to great success.

He regularly performed:

4 sets of Incline Dumbbell Press, 8-10 reps
3 sets of Bench Press, 8-10 reps
3 sets of Incline Flyes, 8-10 reps
3 sets of Chest Dips until failure
3 sets of Barbell Curls, 8-10 reps
3 sets of Preacher Curls, 8-10 reps

And, on the next day:

3 sets of Deadlifts, 8-10 reps
3 sets of Squats, 8-10 reps
3 sets of Clean and Jerk, 8-10 reps
3 sets of Weighted Pull-ups, 8-10 reps

He improved his chest with dumbbell presses, cable crossovers and incline dumbbell flyes. He improved his arms with heavy EZ-bar and hammer curls, and triceps extensions supersetted with close grip bench presses. He improved his quads with squats, leg presses and lunges. He improved his abs with cable crunches and intense Roman chair and medicine ball mountain work, leading to fantastic obliques and serratus development.

He drank nine glasses of Fiji Natural Artesian water every day. He ate raw eggs, natto, pumpkin seeds and gluten-free quinoa. He took creatine, whey protein, ZMA, grape seed extract, L-arginine, maca, coenzyme Q10, selenium and vitamin E. He took monoatomic gold supplements which improved the production of red blood cells in his bone marrow and also conferred mild psychic abilities, allowing him to perceive Reptilian influence in human affairs.

"Gaurav you are getting too shredded when you should be focusing on other things in life such as finding a serious job and a nice girl," Gaurav's father yelled at him one night.

"Shut up Dad I don't have anything to learn from you and I will not stop getting shredded," Gaurav fired back with extreme disdain. Gaurav's father broke into tears as he realized that Gaurav had already surpassed him in every way.

After reaching his finance and fitness goals, Gaurav moved on to other areas of his life. He improved his fashion by hiring a personal stylist. He improved his vision to 20/15 with LASIK surgery. He improved his dental brilliance with regular whitening treatments. He improved his height with human growth hormone and arched insteps. He improved his pelvic floor strength with kegel exercises. He improved his penile length and rigidity with a Phallosan traction device and a VED pump. He improved his facial dynamics with the Starecta method, adding some much-needed symmetry. When his hairline began to recede, he improved it with spironolactone cream and topical RU58841. He improved his odor with Creed Aventus cologne.

He improved his mindfulness with pranayama and Vedantic meditation. He improved his existential authenticity through encounter therapy and spontaneous radical action. He improved his social skills with the Interpersonal Dynamics DVD Master Course from Social_Eclipse, a well-known digital nomad life coach.

He improved his reflexes by paying a small child named Grover, who had been born in an impoverished neighborhood, to follow him from a distance and hurl a spiked reaction ball at his head whenever the impulse struck.

He improved his Amharic pronunciation with regular trips to Addis Ababa and assiduous recitation of the poetry of Mengistu Lemma.

He improved his whistling by attending a bootcamp run by Petyr "Whistlin' Pete" Ferenczi, a Hungarian immigrant who was regarded as the most diabolically versatile and tuneful whistler in the northern hemisphere.

He improved his ability to visualize six-dimensional Calabi-Yau manifolds through an exhaustive study of quintic polynomials over projective complex hyperplanes and their decompositions compatible with local Zariski topology.

He improved his understanding of Aesthetics by reading Walter Pater and watching Zyzz videos on YouTube.

Gaurav realized that all these improvements had the potential to result in narcissism from the increased validation he was receiving as he systematically achieved his goals. In order to combat this, he took pains to pump his humility through regular contact with those whose life circumstances had not allowed them to advance as rapidly as he had. By scrolling through Facebook for hours at a time, he gained a sense of the overwhelming injustice present in the world. The horrors of racism, misogyny, transphobia, ableism and political incompetence encouraged him to keep a vigilant mindset and educate himself on intersectionality. He worried sometimes that he was slipping from wokeness into mere performative woke baeness, and he made certain to increase his monetary contributions to various socially progressive Kickstarter and Patreon projects and pages.

As Gaurav's compassion increased, a corresponding charisma/conviviality imparted a ready ease to his dealings with others. His social life, which had once seemed stillborn, now flourished beyond anything he could previously have imagined. Gaurav decided that rather than accept conventional monogamy, he would choose a polyamorous lifestyle that would allow him to maintain multiple simultaneous long-term relationships. He realized this was a difficult path that would require total honesty and transparency. By the time he turned twenty-three he had fathered six children: one with Mylene, a Filipina nurse he had met online and regularly visited in Manila; three with Berneece, a stripper from the Eldorado Lounge who was saving money to start her own cosmetics business; one with Marielle, a paralegal he had met at the gym; and one with Emilohi, a Nigerian PHD student at the University of Maryland. Gaurav promised to be a major presence in the lives of his children and to support them both emotionally and financially. And as they were all male, he swore they would grow up shielded from toxic masculinity, able to explore any roles or identities they desired without fear of censure from restrictive and essentialist gender ideologies.

One evening, as he was managing his PayPal accounts and examining some erotic photos Mylene had sent him, Gaurav realized that all of his self-development had been leading up to the present moment. His daily training and business routines had given him a life of overwhelming abundance, and when he considered the future, it seemed that there were no limits to what he might achieve. The realization welled up within him, and a novel cognitive event took place. It felt as if his neocortex had been replaced with a small mound of lemon sherbet, every atom of which vibrated with endless possibility. This fizzing lump of Nowness connected him with all high achievers in all times and places. It was as if a river of tiny tingling high fives was flowing along his synapses.

Gaurav stood on his tiptoes and hopped in place until the effect subsided. For 6.7 seconds he had achieved total quantum mindset.

Shortly afterwards, he checked his Gmail inbox and noticed a message from Social_Eclipse, the digital nomad life coach whose DVD Master Course he had studied and implemented with zestful credulity.

What up GG,

Just thought I'd hit you up with a legit inner circle offer as you've definitely earned it. You're one of the most consistently PRESENT people I know and over the past two or three years the entire Interpersonal Dynamics crew has watched you go from already pretty dynamite to basically plutonium gun-type fission weapon level social awareness. Your business is ON POINT and you seem to be holding it down with the multi-LTRs like a beast. Now it's time for you to take the next step as we'd all love to bounce ideas off you and hear your input. We've got our own place we're all renting in Phnom Penh and we call it the Workstation. It's our hot spot for completing next level projects. So come on down to Cambodia and plug yourself into the matrix! Entire crew is young rich fit super motivated and mindful geniuses etc. And we have pizza with weed on it. Let me know when you've booked your flight.

Social_Eclipse Zeke

Gaurav felt more excited than he had in a long time. Somewhat impulsively, he called Social_Eclipse on Skype. Zeke answered immediately, and Gaurav recognized his outline as it popped into view, a lanky entity in a dark blue collared shirt from American Eagle, with sharp green eyes and thick black slicked-back hair. He was seated at an enormous wooden table, and Gaurav could see several other young men next to him who were also staring intently into their MacBooks. Behind them, a reasonably shredded cis-gender Caucasian male was having furious sex with a young Khmer woman, while a different woman, who looked vaguely Honduran, masturbated with a large black dildo. Next to them, a shirtless young man was playing with a cup-and-ball toy and appeared to be attempting some kind of complicated trick. Everyone in the room looked friendly, healthy and motivated.

"What up Zeke, hope I'm not interrupting any-thing," Gaurav said.

"Not at all, thanks for the fast response," Social_Eclipse said. "Not much to add but get your ass down here as soon as possible."

"Booking my ticket right away. Guess it's time for me to become a digital nomad after all."

"Then my job is done, GG. You know there are digital nomads and digital nomadic herders like me."

"Um, what?"

"Digital nomadic herders are digital nomads who encourage other people to become digital nomads, in effect herding them like a nomadic Dokpa herder herds Tibetan yaks. We try to encourage 9-5 types to pack it up and achieve what we call MGM or Migratory Grazing Mindset. Countries with slightly less than

22

first world economies are great places to develop your online business and get cheap drugs and sex, I mean you can go on a budget rampage and it's all good."

"Sounds like an exciting business opportunity that would allow me to extend my personal brand," Gaurav remarked sagaciously.

"That's exactly what it is. Exactly."

The young man seated next to Social_Eclipse now leaned into view. His skin was intensely pale and his hair had been buzzed to a fine shadow. His eyes were wide as he raised a transparent plastic cup for Gaurav to see. Inside was a dark pink paste.

The man said, "New kind of ice cream. Halfway between soft serve and regular. With a bit of a crunch to it like the good kind of freezer burn. This is not normal ice cream and it's happening now. Only two flavors, hazelnut fudge and salted watermelon. That's it, there won't be any others. It's finished. You need to try it and share it everywhere."

"I want this ice cream and I certainly need it in my life," Gaurav said.

"I'm Karol originally from Poland and I invented the ice cream."

"Karol I think I can trade you something for it when I get there. I have some absolutely sick vegan life hacks, like using organic peanut butter to clean a mirror. I don't think you've encountered these particular vegan hacks before."

"It sounds good, Gaurav. We're all waiting for you here at the Workstation."

"Peace out bros I will be there soon," Gaurav said.

Karol nodded, and then Social_Eclipse made a nonchalant hand gesture that signified he would forthwith terminate the Skype call without any protracted farewells.

Gaurav immediately booked a flight to Cambodia, and two months later he touched down at Phnom Penh International Airport. It was the rainy season, wet and hot. Social_Eclipse and several other members of the crew came out to meet him. Gaurav recognized Karol; also present was Mark, the young man Gaurav had noticed playing with the cup-and-ball toy over Skype. Karol was an experimental chef and lifecaster. Mark was a marketer who marketed marketing techniques to marketers who marketed marketing techniques to marketers. Fist bumps were exchanged, and Gaurav was conveyed to the Workstation, whose central room was larger than he had expected. The round wooden table seated nearly twenty people, and Gaurav noticed that several of them were slumped over their MacBooks with their faces down and arms outstretched, as if they were swimming in their seats. Now and then one of them would spasmodically flail his arms and strike his keyboard with the side of his fist, as if he were performing an avant-garde percussion piece.

"What are these bros doing?" Gaurav asked.

"Writing code while running psychedelics. You know what they say—code while tripping balls, then fix errors while coming down on benzos," Mark explained.

"You mean like microdosing LSD before programming?"

"Microdosing is Silicon Valley bullshit. We're all about crash and mash, or macrodosing."

"Uhhh . . . ?"

"Shulgin Level 4 shit. Run DPT+Syrian Rue+ MDMA+2CB then blaze Kandy Kush at the four-hour mark and come down with some benzos. Then immediately eat 100 datura seeds and start mashing the keyboard. Crash and mash, son."

Social_Eclipse said, "Also try daturading or day trading while on datura. You don't know where you are but somehow you get really good at predicting currencies."

"The other day I crashed and mashed and created a new gender-neutral cryptocurrency," Karol said.

"Sounds dope," Gaurav said. "Everyone here is mad present in the moment and I am reminded of Eckhart Tolle's classic work *The Power of Now*. I feel like we've all stopped identifying with the pain-body and moved on to immersing ourselves in the radiant joy of Being."

Social_Eclipse looked at Gaurav in an arch and almost paternalistic way.

"There's nothing WRONG with that of course," he said. "But let me put it this way. Your average 9-5er is so locked into his or her wage slavery that living in the Now seems like a high level of realization. But let's think about it a little more. And since you've taken the time to come out here, I'd like to share a little philosophy we call The Power of Then and Soon. Next level mental shareware for those already running neurological Creative Commons, if you take my meaning."

"Yes lay that shit out," Gaurav said.

"Eckhart Tolle's philosophy is okay if you're still in high school and masturbating to cam girls all the time while wondering why the world isn't recognizing your greatness yet," Social_Eclipse elaborated.

"The problem is he's got it backwards. There is not really any present moment or state of immediate Being . . . it's more like there is *only* a past and *only* a future. There is no moment."

"Yeah," Mark broke in. "In a lot of ways, trying to pin down and enter the Now is like trying to pin down and enter a teenage boy who's completely covered in olive oil. He's a wriggly, slippery sort of creature and will just as soon squirm out of your arms when you're trying to get him on his back and take a good look at him."

Gaurav saw that the Now was, in fact, like a laughing teenage boy covered in olive oil who couldn't be pinned down by an older man, regardless of that man's life achievements.

Mark said, "You want to spread the Now out and take a good look at it, just like you might want to spread open the oil-drenched Icelandic teenager and see what he's got inside him, so to speak. But the Now tells you it thought of you only as a mentor and didn't want that kind of relationship. This is one way the Now is kind of entitled and basically a young asshole without much reciprocity. You understand where I'm going with this Gaurav?"

"Yes I am getting intense value from this conversation," Gaurav acknowledged.

Karol said, "Also not to be throwing shade but Eckhart Tolle kind of looks like a turtle with low T that has been dipped in white privilege and he doesn't have very good phreaking skills to scam payphones in 1981, plus it doesn't seem like he is very good at polyamorous skateboarding; I mean he is not exactly routinely executing savage ollies with a team of thicc clean-living clever level-headed lovers from Honduras. I am sure he COULD do those things if he applied himself but he is just not that motivated. I don't know about you but I want a life of free payphone calls and non-monogamous ollies."

"The point is, focus on the Then and the Soon," Social_Eclipse said. "Where you've been, and where you're headed. It's the only realistic way to live. If it helps, I could get you a 'There is no moment' shirt from my online store. And as far as reading material goes, I advise sticking to texts such as Paulo Coelho's *The Alchemist* aka the crowning achievement of Brazilian literature. I mean João Guimarães Rosa and Clarice Lispector are okay but they didn't exactly drop *The Alchemist* on an unsuspecting public, if you catch my drift."

Mark said, "If Paulo was a breakfast cereal I would douse him in milk and use him to start my day."

Gaurav nodded and updated his worldview.

He spent the rest of the day wandering around the Workstation, eating cheap delivery meals from Foodpanda and discussing startups with some of the other life coaches. Towards evening he noticed that several of those present had gathered around a single laptop and were watching Malcolm Gladwell giving a TED Talk on YouTube. Gladwell was discussing his novel interpretation of the fight between David and Goliath. David, Gladwell explained, was not really an underdog as the conventional interpretation had it.

"Looks like Gladwell is dropping some counterintuitive knowledge that could resonate with my core values," Gaurav speculated to himself. "Gladwell has written numerous books on interesting topics and is a respected and popular journalist."

Just then he felt the buzzing vibration of an incoming call on his iPhone. It was Marielle, the mother of his son Pradeep. She wanted to discuss a bully who had been bothering Pradeep, as well as her own recent stresses at work.

"Sorry I am a bit busy watching TED Talks with my digital nomad life coach friends and cannot provide emotional labor at the moment kthxbye," Gaurav explained, and hit End Call.

As he turned back to the laptop, he sensed a repetitive movement out of the corner of his eye. Glancing over, he saw that Karol had unzipped his pants and was masturbating with a steady, unhurried rhythm.

"Purely non-sexual," Karol said, noticing Gaurav's scrutiny and glancing over for a moment before redirecting his attention to YouTube. "Just, sometimes I become dangerously captivated by the power of TED and demand physical release."

Onscreen, Malcolm Gladwell was describing the probable nature of the slingshot used by David. A stream of tremendous stringy clots like a pearly liquid octopus blasted out of Karol's penis and puddled across the floor.

"Damn that is a lot of semen," Gaurav commented. "Got anybody hacks to increase overall load? I feel like my volume is decent for my age but I want to be firing heavier ammunition if possible."

Karol took out a small packet of tissues and wiped up his fluids. "I get my volume up by eating four stalks of celery every day, a cup of walnuts, fifteen oysters and occasionally a small carob candy. Also try L-carnitine, ginseng and lecithin."

"Sweet, I will take this information on board and hopefully kick my vesicles into beast mode," Gaurav remarked.

"Yes remember they are the tamed yet still occasionally wilful horses and you are the charioteer yanking them any direction you like," Karol said. "At first they may resent your control but eventually they will learn who is the true master."

Gaurav looked at Karol and sensed an ineffable bond of trust forming between them. "Bro I would like to thank you for giving me this info by promoting that new kind of ice cream you mentioned. I can hop onto my Twitch account and talk it up to everyone. I am pretty well-known as an influencer and I'm sure I can get it to go viral. I'll also do a YouTube video and some SEO work for you."

"Thank you Gaurav, I can tell you are a gentleman of probity and severe personal accountability. I will not hesitate to provide you with as much of the hazelnut fudge and salted watermelon flavors as you require for these upcoming endeavors."

"Right on. BTW are you guys intersectional feminists? I'm trying to pump my understanding of the role structural inequalities and class dynamics play in perpetuating the patriarchy and if possible please allow me to add you on Snapchat."

"Yes we are always on that grind," Karol said.

Over the next few weeks Gaurav adjusted to life in Cambodia. He visited Angkor Wat, smoked marijuana, had numerous sexual encounters with locals and tourists alike, attended an EDM club event and discussed various projects with the Workstation crew. After an intense brainstorming session, he and Karol named the new ice cream 'Crunch Frost.' With the help of some compellingly-edited videos and Gaurav's digital marketing skills, they were quickly able to monetize it.

One day Gaurav got the feeling that it was time to go back to America. He had forged invaluable personal and professional connections and gained knowledge of numerous new fields at the Workstation, but he missed his family and friends, and he sensed that he needed to return to a familiar environment to apply some of the lessons he had learned. The Workstation was the ultimate mastermind group he had been looking for, and he vowed to visit it again when he had made sufficient life progress.

"I wish I could stick around, but it's time for me to bounce," he announced one morning.

"No worries GG," Social_Eclipse said. "We're all on the move, all the time. That's what it means to be a digital nomad. I'm sure we'll meet again."

Gaurav and Social_Eclipse performed a largely improvised yet undeniably convoluted handshake, then embraced each other for 4.5 seconds. Karol approached and placed a supportive hand on Gaurav's shoulder, then removed it.

When Gaurav arrived back in Baltimore, he realized that it had been more than five years since his life-changing encounter with Giancarlo in Patterson Park. The two had stayed in touch, until Giancarlo had taken a break from pursuing his life goals in order to explore homelessness and prescription opioid abuse. But he was now clean and working in a shoe store while raising a daughter.

Overcome with nostalgia, Gaurav decided to visit the park again and stroll alone in the sunshine while reflecting on his experiences in Cambodia. He put on a tracksuit and headed out at 8 AM, determined to "make the most of the day." As he was walking past the General Casimir Pulaski Monument, a young man with tortoiseshell glasses and a Black Flag T-shirt wheeled himself over and addressed him.

"Aren't you Gaurav from YouTube?" the man asked.

"Yes I am the well-known influencer and digital marketer Gaurav Gupta," Gaurav said. "Add me on Twitter: @gauravgupta420."

"I am more than familiar with your Twitter account which is essentially a compendium of elegant and important thoughts delivered in real-time," the man said. "My name is Enrique and I am a graphic designer."

"What are you up to today bro?" Gaurav asked.

"I'd planned to attend an exhibition of contemporary street art done on skateboard decks at the nearby Anderson Arts Center, until I discovered that the center does not have wheelchair access. As a result I am unable to view the work of young men and women," Enrique lamented. "Because of their failure to implement the principles of universal design, I am literally unable to support local artists."

"It sounds like the organizers of this art exhibition are rather ableist," Gaurav remarked.

"Yes they are shitting fuck ass bastard piss sandwiches with a side order of rubbish," Enrique said. "They are also inconsiderate."

"I was doing some private reflection on my upcoming projects, but now I invite you to join me on my stroll," Gaurav said.

"Thank you Gaurav, it is an honor to spend time with you. BTW do you know any lit parties going on in this area?"

"Yes I am usually attending lit, dope and ill parties that are fucking sick," Gaurav said. "Evidence of my attendance can be accessed digitally on the Instagram platform. I will be hitting up a club event later tonight and I invite you to come along."

The two of them continued on their way, with Gaurav practicing his whistling as they walked. He had made incredible advances since the days of his bootcamp and was now a soloist of almost needlessly technical extravagance. He warbled and trilled his way through the William Tell Overture for a while, breaking off only when he heard the tentative sound of a small boy also attempting to whistle, as he did not want his obviously superior skills to shame this amateur whose range and register were embarrassingly limited in comparison with his own.

"Shit that was some intense whistling," Enrique said. "Hey check it out, something is going down over there . . ."

Gaurav looked in the direction of the boat lake and saw that a small crowd had gathered around two young men who were hunched over what appeared to be a mechanical contraption with something furry struggling at its center. When he and Enrique moved closer, they saw that it was a beagle with tan and white fur, and that the "contraption" was actually several distinct objects; each of the dog's legs had been clamped in one of four Wilton 3VB Vacuum Base Vises. The animal seemed to be suffering greatly, constrained by the cruel devices which one of the men was tightening while his partner filmed the scene with a GoPro camera. Both men were in their early twenties and appeared reasonably shredded. They wore matching T-shirts bearing a cartoon image of a saw. Gaurav saw that the first man, who wore a backwards Ravens baseball cap, held such a tool in his free hand.

"Hello I am Gaurav," said Gaurav as he approached. "Who are you and what are you doing with this canine?"

The man in the Ravens cap turned to him. "My name is Cid spelled with a C like in Final Fantasy although when I was born my mother was not aware of this electronic corporate role-playing product from the distant Orient. I was named after Rodrigo Díaz de Vivar, the Castilian nobleman and military leader in medieval Spain, referred to by the Moors as El Cid. I have released a number of tracks on Spotify that I would advise you to investigate."

The man with the camera spoke next. He was shorter than his friend, and had a small black star tattooed on his left cheek. "I am Antwan and I am rocking this GoPro for dollars. My hobbies include getting silly rich, maintaining the integrity of my ego fortress and following recent trends in contemporary urban architecture. My favorite painter is Frida Kahlo and my favorite condiment is Heinz ketchup. I am NOT a cat person and do not appreciate the impudence with which some felines conduct themselves."

"I agree that cats are overrated especially by individuals who consider themselves quirky, sensitive or otherwise elevated from the mainstream in an ostensibly self-deprecating but, in fact, rather elitist manner," Gaurav concurred. "It is also the case that Heinz ketchup is the superior condiment. But to return to the matter at hand, it seems you are about to apply a deadly sawing force to this dog."

Cid said, "Yes we are just about to get the video underway and we will be sawing this beagle in half for our YouTube channel and then also sawing off the beagle's head. Just a day ago it was living securely in a rescue shelter, concerned only with its gross animal needs, but now it is about to be confronted with direct experience of the ontological uncertainty that lies beyond death. It will be liberated into Eternity by means of the repetitive sawing motion which I am about to perform."

"I have a companion animal who is a terrier named Hector and I would be rather distraught if someone sawed his head or otherwise damaged his cranium," said Enrique. He turned to Gaurav. "These young YouTubers should not be sawing the animals or otherwise violating their bodily integrity."

Gaurav nodded at his new friend and then turned back to the young men. "Sawing beagles is highly problematic and I would not recommend it, especially not as a means of increasing AdSense revenue if that is the goal. Avoiding gratuitous damage to animals is an essential part of expanding your sphere of empathy and concern. Dogs and other canids are non-human individuals and often feel pain when sawed or otherwise injured."

Cid finished tightening the vises and took a step back. The beagle, realizing that its struggling was only causing it more pain, whined piteously. "This is true but the We Saw Everything Channel is all sawing, all the time. In some videos we saw metal pipes and in others we saw plastic toys. We have even sawn a tire and in our most popular video to date we sawed a box of Oreos. So it is not that we are specifically sawing this dog, it is just that we saw everything and we have had requests to saw a beagle for some time now. It appears that a number of viewers would dearly like to see a small tan and white hound subjected to bisection by means of the cunning and wicked blade of a TEKTON 6832 2-in-1 High-Tension Hacksaw."

Antwan said, "Also cruelty to animals is a good way to attract attention and go viral. Sure people will complain, but then we can do a sincere apology video and generate some backlash clickbait articles to raise our hits. So it's all good . . . we are monetizing our channel and we have nothing with the outcast and the unfit: let them die in their misery. For they feel not. Compassion is the vice of kings: stamp down the wretched and the weak: this is the law of the strong: this is our law and the joy of the world."

Several members of the crowd cheered at this last statement, and Gaurav sensed that they were eager to witness the spectacle of public dog violence which Cid and Antwan had promised. He stepped forward and placed a hand on Cid's shoulder. "Bro, you are a chiseled hominid with outstanding career prospects and it is not right that you are relying on backlash revenue from reckless sawing. I advise you to take advantage of the one infallible tool that will allow you to seize hold of your destiny in an immediate sense with direct and licit results that are certifiably mindblowing. I am speaking of the LinkedIn professional network."

Cid's lineaments manifested what Gaurav had been culturally conditioned to recognize as an expression of skeptical disdain. "I've heard LinkedIn is not what it used to be and is not such a great place to build a digital portrait of myself that emphasizes my employment history."

"This is not the case and, in fact, LinkedIn is a sturdy job hunting cannon that you should not hesitate to wheel out when the going gets competitive," Gaurav advocated convincingly. "Lots of people have killer LinkedIn profiles but you want yours to be utterly homicidal and remorseless, at least in the metaphorical sense of expanding your professional network and alerting possible future employers to the contemporary relevance of your skill set."

Antwan said, "I already have a LinkedIn profile but I don't check it that much because it's just a bunch of assholes in suits posting fake business advice and weird listicles all the time."

"Not updating your LinkedIn profile regularly is a bit like only brushing your teeth every few weeks. In other words, it's bad professional hygiene likely to lead to the equivalent of gum disease of the career, which could make your resume look shriveled and unhealthy, or else not properly padded and displayed."

"Yeah, I tried to update it a few times but didn't get any instant job offers with full health insurance."

"A thorough job search should include identifying at least 100 people not advertising your desired position but with the power to hire you for your target job or create it for you. You need to rock up with intense personal conviction and not just pitch yourself as the best thing since melted butter, but also make an effort to build a relationship with them over several months. You also need to regularly contact your extended personal network to get leads. Don't just throw out a boring resume . . . you need to include collateral material like a white paper, a project portfolio and recommendations from any well-known people you've collaborated with in the past. Also, do substantive follow-ups after interviews. The LinkedIn professional network should be your constant friend and ally."

The crowd had fallen silent, and for a while Cid and Antwan also seemed at a loss for anything to say. The beagle had resumed its struggle to escape, and its intermittent whining took on an imploring tone. Its wide brown eyes were bloodshot orbs of terror.

"Suppose I wanted to put my LinkedIn profile through a bulking phase," Cid said. "What steps could I take to make massive gains in as little time as possible? If what you've been telling me is true, an absolutely jacked profile could lead to more offers from recruiters."

Gaurav said, "Yes the more jacked and shredded yet streamlined and accessible your profile becomes, the more you'll feel at ease with your physicality and not like you're a teenager who's been eating too many sugary carbohydrates from Krispy Kreme and unnecessarily spiking your insulin while becoming jittery and nervous from washing down the glazed chocolate cake doughnut holes with iced skinny vanilla latte after iced skinny vanilla latte as you listen on a vintage Sony Walkman WM-EX672 to "The Everyday World of Bodies" by Rodan, the post-hardcore band from Louisville, Kentucky that broke up in 1995. And the trick to getting more people to look at your LinkedIn profile is almost criminally easy. You don't even need to upgrade to Premium."

"Are you willing to explain this trick to us without immediate monetary recompense?" Antwan asked.

"Yes, I will provide it free of any obligations, financial or otherwise."

Cid and Antwan looked at each other in silence for 8.3 seconds while their faces transitioned through various emotions. At first, they seemed equally bewildered; then, as they carried on a sort of soundless conversation, their expressions progressed towards a look of calm, shared certainty. Antwan gave an almost imperceptible nod and, without a word, Cid reached down and loosened the vises. The beagle had evidently sustained damage to its metatarsals, as its first free steps were staggers leading to a quick collapse. A young girl in a white top and purple shorts emerged from the crowd, picked up the animal and held it in her arms. The beagle licked her face.

"Hit us up with the info," Cid said.

Gaurav nodded, his face serious yet encouraging. "In short, your LinkedIn profile should be compact, content-rich and visually appealing. It should be balanced and symmetrical. First, it's essential to choose a background profile image. It should ideally be a neutral shot of a beautiful workspace, a side view of any office-related objects or computers, or else a relaxing scene from nature. Stock photos are okay for these purposes and of course make sure there are not any small plastic drug bags or vials or an outdated box of cereal or anything else that seems suspicious and could subliminally influence a recruiter or future employer to move away from your profile or otherwise consider you a less than viable candidate. Next up, get a professional profile picture. Look directly at the camera and make sure your clothes are crisp and well-ironed. Posture and jawline prominence are important for displaying basic confidence/competence. If you're not used to attaining conscious awareness of how your jaw is resting, I can recommend some clenching exercises and a free jaw tutorial."

"To be honest my jaw has always been kind of wack," Cid said.

"It is a common problem but can be fixed with some exercises. Anyway, drop some cash on a professional photographer to make sure your picture portrays you as confident, successful, trustworthy, stable and influential. Don't just use a random candid shot with your underwear around your ankles and a half-eaten pomegranate on the nightstand."

"Roger that," Antwan said.

"Then move onto your profile summary and info. It needs to be a personal mission statement that express-es your focus and presents you as a three-dimensional individual with human weaknesses and not just a shuffling mass of organs or some kind of watery car-bon robot moving about blindly without concern for global sustainability or resource management. In order to create a compelling and consistent profile, you need to display raw authenticity, or, in other words, the sin-cere sum totality of your vision, values and voice. And this authenticity cannot be counterfeited, not even if a clone of you was produced from your own DNA, because the clone would lack your experiences and so would not be as authentic even if it watched videos of you in order to imitate your mannerisms and started reading old Tumblr entries where you reposted im-ages of bands like City of Caterpillar alongside selfies and hoped that purple-haired girls would notice your account even though your hair is kind of curly and wouldn't straighten enough to pull off a swooping 'wolf cut' hairstyle which these emotive and confessional girls seem to prefer."

Cid said, "Yes that Tumblr-copying clone would definitely not be as authentic, even if a purple-haired girl with black boots and good facial symmetry noticed his interest in City of Caterpillar."

"So, use the right keywords in your profile to maximize search engine hits," Gaurav continued. "But avoid buzzwords like responsible, strategic, energetic, motivated, enthusiastic, specialized or innovative. Instead you could describe yourself as profligate, dictatorial, monolithic, infectious, magisterial, ineluctable, rectitudinous, epochal or merely apposite. You don't want too little information, or too much. Vague claims of technical expertise should be backed up by specific portfolio examples with links whenever possible. And update your headline. It's the first thing recruiters notice. Normally it will default to your current company and position, but you can customize it, and you definitely should. For example, you could describe yourself as an Extroverted Facilitator with a Passion for Event Orchestration, or a Video Marketing Coordinator with a Sideline in Social Media Analytics. Or a Demographic Infiltrator with an Irrepressible Conscience. Really the possibilities are limitless. And don't forget that the experience section should be an expanded resume, and should include multimedia components, along with mention of any awards you've received."

"You mean the multimedia components will make it easier for recruiters to contact me?" Antwan asked.

"Yes this is incontestably the case," Gaurav averred. "We've talked about the bulking phase, and now for the cutting phase. Filter through your skills and endorsements. Not all of them should make the cut just because someone added them. Think of yourself as a bouncer, and your skills and endorsements as random drunk servicemen attempting to enter the high-class club of your LinkedIn profile. You wouldn't want to let all of them in when not appropriate. In particular, it's not necessary to include taken-for-granted skills like PowerPoint and Microsoft Office. And non-specific endorsements need to go, but recommendations from previous employers are a good way to demonstrate credibility. Be sure to keep your resume on point and don't just include everything you've ever done. You don't want to come off like a Peter Pan whose career is stagnating and who is too careless to prune his history when needed. You want to liposuction your resume to remove the fat, then polish it to a shine. Your LinkedIn profile is sort of like your abs, and you want to keep them shaved and in good condition in case anyone sees them from an angle you're not expecting. You want to get maximum definition in the same way you want a glabrous and well-maintained LinkedIn page that's up to date and doesn't seem carelessly groomed."

"I'm pretty certain I can forcibly siphon out flabby deposits from my employment history by removing irrelevant jobs of grey zone legality," Cid said.

"That is a stellar idea," Gaurav said. "Once you've done all this, you should then turn outwards and follow key leaders and influencers in your industry so that your newsfeed is filled with relevant advice. Your LinkedIn newsfeed is the grapevine of your industry and just like a grapevine it requires temperate weather in order to produce fruit. Post links to any relevant articles connected to your industry, and curate your groups to delete any that aren't helping you. Reach out to old contacts to maintain your professional network. Having too few connections implies you're not interpersonally-focused which is a disastrous no-no in today's human-focused marketplace."

Cid, whose expression had been neutral for some time, was now slowly shaking his head as he broke into a smile. "I feel as if I've just bought a 15 Piece Chicken McNuggets except instead of small mounds of processed meat they're golden nuggets of LinkedIn wisdom."

"And now it's up to you to dip those nuggets in the invigorating sauce carton of conscientious application," Gaurav asseverated. "In other words, dip your nuggets and eat them too. And game LinkedIn like it was a casino with visually-impaired dealers."

Gaurav became aware that several people in the crowd were filming him, and, in fact, Antwan's GoPro had been running the whole time. Enrique, who had inconspicuously departed a few minutes earlier, now returned with a bag full of energy drinks, which he passed out to those present. Cid and Antwan accepted his generosity as they had accepted Gaurav's. Sawing a live dog in public had not been the clever stunt they had hoped it would be, and they felt appropriately chastened.

"Bros let's come in closer," Gaurav said.

Cid and Antwan came forward, and they formed a circle with Gaurav and Enrique, reaching out their hands and placing them on top of each other.

"Now, from this day on we're going to keep self-motivating and we're going to push ourselves to the next level in everything. Let's all keep reaching our performance targets as dynamic, motivated individuals . . . and let's all say it together. No to public dog sawing stunts, and yes to LinkedIn."

The four men threw their hands to the sky. And with hearty and zestful conviction they repeated:

"No to public dog sawing stunts, and yes to LinkedIn!"

THEY TOLD ME TO STOP WHORING
MY SUFFERING AND EAT MORE STEAK

Spontaneous Reincarnation

"Well, this is a fine pickle we've got ourselves in," MacArthur said.

Hirohito looked at MacArthur's pelvis. There was something obscenely womanish about it—its sloping girth and the way the rest of him seemed to follow it as he walked. The pipe jutted from his mouth like a handle.

Hirohito looked down at his Mickey Mouse watch.

Café

They were sitting in a café. They didn't have any yen, and from time to time the waiter would wander over and bother them.

"We need jobs," Hirohito said.

"We don't have any qualifications," MacArthur said.

"We need jobs."

"I am the Supreme Commander of the Allied Powers. You are the Emperor of Japan."

44

"We're not, anymore. We're nothing."

"I am not nothing," MacArthur said. "Every man has been put here for a reason."

Newspaper

"Hotel staff," Hirohito said, and put down the newspaper. They'd found it near the trash. They were sitting next to a man in a purple blanket. From time to time the suits would toss him coins.

"Management?"

"No . . ."

"Well, reception?"

"Room service. Transport, cleaning, things like that."

"Chambermaids," MacArthur said. "We're going to be chambermaids."

"Hotel staff," Hirohito said.

Employment

Hirohito picked a used condom from the floor. There was a knock on the door.

The woman asked for extra towels and Hirohito took them from his trolley. He put his hands at his sides.

He gave a little bow after each service he performed.

The woman didn't thank him.

Everyone was taller than him, he thought.

When MacArthur walked down the hallway, he shambled and slouched. He seemed to push the trolley with his stomach.

Piece of Shit

"This hotel is a piece of shit," Arturo said. "They should burn it to the ground."

He handed Hirohito a tin of biscuits. They always took coffee breaks in the check-out rooms when the supervisor wasn't around.

"Philippines is better than this," Arturo said.

"I used to be big in the Philippines," MacArthur said.

Encounter

"I'm really really sorry," Reiko said.

She stepped out of the elevator and vomited.

"I'm so, so sorry," she said. "You're going to have to clean that up, right?"

Hirohito looked at her.

Reprimand

"Your hygiene and personal conduct are not up to standard," Mr. Kaji said.

"What are you talking about?" MacArthur said.

"We have standards at this hotel," Mr. Kaji said. "Our cleaning staff are expected to dress neatly, and carry themselves with a certain bearing. We do not . . . slouch."

Direction

"Thanks so much for the towels," Reiko said.

"Is there anything else you'd like?"

"That's fine . . . oh, I was wondering. How can I get to Asakusa from here?"

"Would you like me to show you? I can show you."

"You mean . . ."

"I'll be finished soon," Hirohito said.

Dissatisfaction

"What the hell are we doing here, Arturo," MacArthur said. "A couple of guys like us."

"Do you have any more creamers in your trolley," Arturo said. "I'm out of creamers."

Interpersonal Relationship

"You don't think I'm too old?" Hirohito said.

"I like old guys," Reiko said.

Ten minutes passed.

"Are you being serious?" Hirohito said.

Tokyo Disneyland

"We should all go to Tokyo Disneyland," Reiko said.

They went there.

"I can't understand any of this," MacArthur said. "Goofy is supposed to speak English, for fuck's sake. Donald Duck is the only one that is making any sense."

Nostalgia

They were alone in the apartment.

"I think I want to get back into the army," MacArthur said.

"They're not going to let you do anything with Korea," Hirohito said.

"If they had of trusted me, this situation wouldn't even exist now."

Hirohito got another beer. "No one believes I'm a god anymore," he said.

"I don't see why they wouldn't trust me," MacArthur said.

Hirohito's face went crooked. "You were going too far in Korea," he said.

"I wasn't going too far."

"You were going too far. You were going to destroy the world. You destroyed the world . . ."

"The people need a firm hand."

"No one cared when I died. Because of you, the divine spirit of the Yamato people was destroyed."

"Nonsense. I showed you the democratic way of life. The people of this country live in peace and harmony now, just like the American people."

Hirohito got up and left.

"Hey . . . come on . . . I didn't mean it," MacArthur said.

Conflict

"Are you going to come out of there, or not?"

"Say your Occupation destroyed Japan, you were wrong about Korea, and the Yamato people are a divine race."

"Look . . . maybe I got a little carried away with Korea . . ."

"Say it!"

Intervention

"Hirohito is a little bastard," MacArthur said. "I'm not talking to him anymore."

Reiko went over to Hirohito's room.

"MacArthur is an imperialist swine," Hirohito said. "I'm not talking to him anymore."

Reconciliation

"This is a dead country," Hirohito said. "The entire world is dead."

"But we're alive," MacArthur said.

"Why?"

"I don't know. Maybe the Lord Jesus Christ has more work for us to do."

"I like Mickey Mouse," Hirohito said.

Eviction

"Well, hell, we only make so much," MacArthur said.

"Reiko's parents don't like me," Hirohito said. "So we can't stay there. I can't stay there."

"Why not?"

"They were student activists in the 70s," Hirohito said. "They called me a relic. To my face."

Street

"I was lying when I said I wasn't a god," Hirohito said. "I am the father of the nation."

"You're insane," MacArthur said. "There's only one God, and his name is Jesus Christ."

"I am a god," Hirohito said. "I am the descendant of Amaterasu-o-mi-kami. No one can look at my real face!"

His eyes went wet. The night stretched before him, jeweled.

MacArthur lifted his leg.

Empire

"The supervisor is an asshole," MacArthur said. "We shouldn't trust her, she's got two faces."

"I was already fired," Hirohito said. "I don't know how to clean, really."

Reiko placed another blanket over them. She'd already taken MacArthur's temperature. He was coughing a little.

"Reiko, let's start another country somewhere," Hirohito said. "Come with me and be my empress. We won't tell anyone where we are. We'll be invisible. In our empire there will be no televisions, no hotels . . ."

"I'm sorry," Reiko said. "I have to study."

"I am issuing an Imperial Rescript," Hirohito said. "Dissolving your university."

"My parents . . ."

"I will issue a new Imperial Rescript, dissolving your family."

"I like my family."

"They're dissolved," Hirohito said. "I am the only person you are allowed to love. By Imperial Rescript."

"Don't listen to him, he's crazy," MacArthur said.

"I am issuing an Imperial Rescript that will dissolve you, MacArthur. You no longer exist."

"I'm in all the books," MacArthur said.

"I will dissolve them," Hirohito said. "I dissolve history. I dissolve this country. We are now living on an island. There are only three people here."

"I'm leaving," Reiko said.

"An Imperial Rescript compels you to stay."

"They should have let me go with Korea," MacArthur said. "I don't understand why they didn't trust me."

Reiko left.

"Where's she going, do you think?" MacArthur said.

"There's nowhere for her to go," Hirohito said. "The borders of my empire are well patrolled."

"We should find a new job," MacArthur said. "I'm thinking of getting back into the army, but . . ."

The man with the purple blanket came over.

"You can't stay here," he said. "This is my place."

"I dissolved you," Hirohito said. "You don't exist."

The man kicked him.

"Give me your watch," he said.

"I need my watch," Hirohito said. "I use it to tell time."

"What time is it now?"

"Time is running backwards," Hirohito said. "Soon we'll be arriving in the 20s."

"No Mickey Mouse then," MacArthur said.

"Mickey Mouse is allowed in my empire," Hirohito said.

"Can I join your empire?" the man with the purple blanket said.

"I already told you, you don't exist," Hirohito said. "I've dissolved you."

"I have to exist!" the man in the purple blanket said.

"Maybe I should start my own army," MacArthur said.

"Can I join it?" the man in the purple blanket said.

"I think it would be a better idea for you to accept the Lord Jesus Christ first," MacArthur said. "The same goes for you."

"People who don't exist are talking to me," Hirohito said. "I must be going crazy."

THE ITALIAN REALITY

"Herbert! Good God! Is it possible?"

"Yes, my name's Herbert. I think I know your face, too, but I don't remember your name. My memory is very queer."

"Don't you recollect Villiers of Wadham?"

"So it is, so it is. I beg your pardon, Villiers, I didn't think I was begging of an old college friend. Good-night."

"My dear fellow, this haste is unnecessary. My rooms are close by, but we won't go there just yet. Suppose we walk up Shaftesbury Avenue a little way? But how in heaven's name have you come to this pass, Herbert?"

"It's a long story, Villiers, and a strange one too, but you can hear it if you like."

"Come on, then. Take my arm, you don't seem very strong."

The ill-assorted pair moved slowly up Rupert Street; the one in dirty, evil-looking rags, and the other attired in the regulation uniform of a man about town, trim, glossy, and eminently well-to-do. Villiers had emerged from his restaurant after an excellent dinner of many courses, assisted by an ingratiating little flask of Chianti, and, in that frame of mind which was with him almost chronic, had delayed a moment by the door, peering round in the dimly-lighted street in search of those mysterious incidents and persons with which the streets of London teem in every quarter and every hour. Villiers prided himself as a practised explorer of such obscure mazes and byways of London life, and in this unprofitable pursuit he displayed an assiduity which was worthy of more serious employment. Thus he stood by the lamp-post surveying the passers-by with undisguised curiosity, and with that gravity known only to the systematic diner, had just enunciated in his mind the formula:

"London has been called the city of encounters; it is more than that, it is the city of Resurrections," when these reflections were suddenly interrupted by a piteous whine at his elbow, and a deplorable appeal for alms. He looked around in some irritation, and with a sudden shock found himself confronted with the embodied proof of his somewhat stilted fancies. There, close beside him, his face altered and disfigured by poverty and disgrace, his body barely covered by greasy ill-fitting rags, stood his old friend Charles Herbert, who had matriculated on the same day as himself, with whom he had been merry and wise for twelve revolving terms. Different occupations and varying interests had interrupted the friendship, and it was six years since Villiers had seen Herbert; and now he looked upon this wreck of a man with grief and dismay, mingled with a certain inquisitiveness as to what dreary chain of circumstances had dragged him down to such a doleful pass. Villiers felt together with compassion all the relish of the amateur in mysteries, and congratulated himself on his leisurely speculations outside the restaurant.

They walked on in silence for some time, and more than one passer-by stared in astonishment at the unaccustomed spectacle of a well-dressed man with an unmistakable beggar hanging on to his arm, and, observing this, Villiers led the way to an obscure street in Soho. Here he repeated his question.

"How the fuck did it happen, Herbert? I always understood you would succeed to an excellent position in Dorsetshire. Did your old man disinherit you? Surely not?"

"No, Villiers; I came into all the property at my poor father's death; he died a year after I left Oxford. He was a very good father to me, and I mourned his death sincerely enough. But you know what young men are; a few months later I came up to town and went a good deal into society. And by society I mean clubs where I could practice my considerable para-para dance skills. Of course I had excellent introductions, and I managed to enjoy myself very much in a harmless sort of way. I played a little, certainly, but never for heavy stakes, and the contests I entered brought me in money—only a few pounds, you know, but enough to pay for cigars and such petty pleasures. It was in my second season that the tide turned. Of course you have heard of my marriage?"

"No, I never heard anything about it."

"Yes, I married, Villiers. I met a girl, a girl of the most wonderful and most strange beauty, coming out of Atom in Shibuya one night. I cannot tell you her age; I never knew it, but, so far as I can guess, I should think she must have been about nineteen when I made her acquaintance. My friends had come to know her at

Florence; she told them she was an orphan, the child of an English father and an Italian mother, and she charmed them as she charmed me. The first time I saw her was on the psychedelic trance floor. I was standing by the door talking to a friend, when suddenly above the hum and babble of conversation I heard a voice which seemed to thrill to my heart. She was singing an Italian song. I was introduced to her that evening, and in three months I married Helen. Villiers, that woman, if I can call her woman, corrupted my soul. You, Villiers, you may think you know life, and London, and what goes on day and night in this dreadful city; for all I can say you may have heard the talk of the vilest, but I tell you that you can have no conception of what I know, not in your most fantastic, hideous dreams can you have imaged forth the faintest shadow of what I have heard—and seen. Yes, seen. I have seen the incredible, such horrors that even I myself sometimes stop in the middle of the street and ask whether it is possible for a man to behold such things and live. In a year, Villiers, I was a broken man, in body and soul—in body and soul."

"But your property, Herbert? You had land in Dorset."

"I sold all that shit—everything."

"And the money?"

"She took it all. Bitch ruined me, Villiers! Before this I had a 401k plan and a two-car garage. I had a flatscreen plasma television and a comprehensive collection of 90s J-pop; I mean I was shithoarding 90s J-vinyl. All of it's gone, Villiers."

"And then she left you?"

"Yes; she disappeared one night. I don't know where she went, but I am sure if I saw her again it would kill me. The rest of my story is of no interest; sordid misery, that is all. You may think, Villiers, that I have exaggerated and talked for effect; but I have not told you half. I could tell you certain things which would convince you, but you would never know a happy day again. You would pass the rest of your life, as I pass mine, a haunted man, a man who has seen hell."

"Come on Herbert, you gotta tell me more of this shit. I honestly don't know what the fuck you're talking about."

"Serious?"

"Yeah, shit, you're being hell vague."

"I dunno. This shit is inconceivable, unspeakable. I can't tell you any more."

"Herbert, don`t be a little bitch. Tell the fucking story."

"Okay. The night of the wedding, I found myself sitting in her bedroom in the hotel, listening to her talk. She was sitting up in bed, and I listened to her as she spoke in her beautiful voice, spoke of things which even now I would not dare whisper in the blackest night, though I stood in the midst of a wilderness. Then she started trying to test my dance skills. She was like, 'Herbert, your skills are getting weak, can you touch this shit?' Then she started in with this really weak ass routine that even Ken Maeda wouldn`t touch. I was like 'Helen, just stop. You're half-Italian, and Italians can't dance.'"

"They seriously fucking can't. God dammit Herbert . . . we've been landed—forever, or so it seems!—with those dull-eyed, olive-skinned chocolate munchers and garlic crushers who are not the least bit English but rather Italian. In short, we've been overrun by the Latin race—cocky, treacherous, over-emotional imbeciles one and all that can go to the Devil for all I care!"

Herbert raised his eyebrows.

"My, my," he said, laughing. "Your remarks prove to me that you are interested in 'our own, our native land.' I should never have suspected it of you."

"Of course you wouldn't," said Villiers, lighting a cigarette. "As has so often been said, 'My own, my native land is wherever I happen to feel at home.' Now I don't feel at home except with the people of the North. But I interrupted you. Let's get back to the subject. What were you saying?"

"Okay, yeah. Helen was pissing me off, so I was like 'Bitch, stop.' Then I started busting some tight ass moves. So Helen was like, 'Okay Herbert, but what about *this* shit?' Then she takes this *door* out of her pocket . . ."

"Uhhh, what the fuck?"

"Yeah like this miniature fucking *door*. And it gets real big all of a sudden and opens, and this Italian monk comes out. He's like, 'Follow me, Herbert . . .'"

"You told him to fuck off, right?"

"Yeah. But he comes out and grabs me and pulls me through the door. And on the other side it's nothing but Italians. I mean it's some kind of Italian church with like ten thousand Italians gathered together and all chanting to the Pope, who's standing at the head of the altar."

"Shit . . ."

"The Pope looked at me and said, 'Italo-disco can't be stopped. Soon you'll be dancing to even more Giorgio Moroder-ripoff shit.'"

"Impossible!" Villiers exclaimed.

"I said that too," Herbert continued. "And then the Pope said, 'When Italo-disco hits lost their popularity in Europe, the Japanese market forced Italian and German producers to evolve the sound to what ended up under the term 'Eurobeat' and later Super Eurobeat and Eurobeat Flash. Those music styles, under the term Eurobeat, are sold only in Japan due to the Para Para culture there. Italian producers are still producing songs for the Japanese (super) Eurobeat market in the 2000s. This evolving sound of Italo-disco involves a much higher BPM, as well as more rapid synth-lines and faster vocals. The genre itself upped the BPM in the late 80s, all the way into the 2000s.'"

"Good God!" Villiers shouted.

"Then . . . the organ broke out overhead with a blare. A dazzling light filled the church, blotting the altar from my eyes. The Italians faded away, the arches, the vaulted roof vanished. I raised my seared eyes to the fathomless glare, and I saw the black stars hanging in the heavens: and the wet winds from Lake Como chilled my face. And now, far away, over leagues of tossing cloud-waves, I saw the moon dripping with spray; and beyond, the towers of Rome rose behind the moon. And now I heard *his* voice, rising, swelling, thundering through the flaring light, and as I fell, the radiance increasing, increasing, poured over me in waves of flame. Then I sank into the depths, and I heard the Pope whispering to my soul: 'It is a fearful thing to fall into the hands of the living God!'"

Villiers looked at him for a long time.

"Fuck all Italians they are the worst country in Europe inferior even to Belgium," he said at last.

NOT SUPER IMPORTANT
RAINING DEAD

The man laid one hand on the paperboy's shoulders, then grasped the boy's chin and turned his face slowly from one side to the other. The boy shrank back uneasily.

"Say! What's the big idea?"

The boy's voice was shrill; inside the café it was suddenly very quiet.

The man said slowly: "I can't stop thinking about vaginas."

All along the counter the men laughed. The boy, who had scowled and sidled away, did not know what to do. He looked over the counter at Wong, and Wong watched him with a weary, brittle jeer. The boy tried to laugh also. But the man was serious and sad.

"I did not mean to tease you, son," he said. "Sit down and smoke some crack with me. There is something I have to explain."

Cautiously, out of the corner of his eye, the paperboy questioned the men along the counter to see what he should do. But they had gone back to their beer or their breakfast and did not notice him. Wong put a glass pipe on the counter.

"Take monster hits boi," Wong said. "This senior citizen is running a tab."

The paperboy slid himself up onto the stool. His ear beneath the upturned flap of the helmet was very small and red. The man was nodding at him soberly. "It is important," he said. Then he reached into his hip pocket and brought out something which he held up in the palm of his hand for the boy to see.

"Look very carefully," he said.

The boy stared, but there was nothing to look at very carefully. The man held in his big, grimy palm a photograph. It was a desert landscape, and in the air, suspended by itself, was a soft pink vulva, its prepuce and labia emitting a steady radiance.

"See?" the man asked.

The boy nodded and the man placed another picture in his palm. The vulva was floating above a beach now, and its glow seemed stronger, causing the picture to look overexposed.

"Got a good look?" He leaned over closer and finally asked: "You ever seen that before?"

The boy sat motionless, staring slantwise at the man. "Not so I know of."

"Very well." The man blew on the photographs and put them back into his pocket. "That was a vagina."

"Your mother's?" the boy asked.

Slowly the man shook his head. He pursed his lips as though about to whistle and answered in a long-drawn way: "Nuuu—" he said. "I will explain."

The beer on the counter before the man was in a large brown mug. He did not pick it up to drink. Instead he bent down and, putting his face over the rim, he rested there for a moment. Then with both hands he tilted the mug and sipped.

"Some night you'll go to sleep with your big nose in a mug and drown," said Wong. "Prominent transient drowns in beer. I will Instagram the fuck out of your corpse."

The paperboy tried to signal to Wong. While the man was not looking he screwed up his face and worked his mouth to question soundlessly: "Drunk?" But Wong only raised his eyebrows and turned away to distribute more pipes.

The man pushed the mug away from him, straightened himself, and folded his loose crooked hands on the counter. His face was sad as he looked at the paperboy. He did not blink, but from time to time the lids closed down with delicate gravity over his dark brown eyes. It was nearing dawn and the boy shifted the weight of the paper sack.

"I am talking about vaginas," the man said. "With me they are a science."

The boy half slid down from the stool. But the man raised his forefinger, and there was something about him that held the boy and would not let him go away.

"Twelve years ago, I was traveling in outer Mongolia. At that time I was a DJ at one of China's hottest nightclubs, but my life wasn't satisfying. I had everything you're supposed to want: socks, shoes, influence. But it wasn't enough. Spiritually, I was empty. There was a hole, an absence in me, which craved God. Are you listening to me, son? Without God, we are nothing. But at that time I knew nothing, only that something was wrong. So I retreated into the desert. For days I walked alone, wandering with no destination in mind, hoping that the universe would take care of me. As my supplies dwindled, I faced the sun and prayed to the sky for enlightenment. When I looked down again, a vagina was floating in the air above me, the same one you saw in the picture, transmitting waves of calm. I asked it what was the meaning of my life. And then a voice sounded from within the vagina. 'All time and space is slowly moving towards the Absolute,' it told me. 'In the name of thrice-great Hermes, I proclaim the Aquarian Age . . .'"

The man paused.

"The macrocosm is contained within the microcosm. There is no time, every instant is proof of divinity. We are all parts of God—pancreatic cells, perhaps. I realized that was what the vagina was trying to tell me."

He tightened his blurred, rambling voice and said:

"I took care of that vagina. I loved it. Yes . . . I loved it. I thought also that it loved me. It had all the home comforts and luxuries. It never crept into my brain that it was not satisfied. But do you know what happened?"

"Mgneeow!" said Wong.

The man did not take his eyes from the boy's face. "The vagina disappeared. I came in one night and the house was empty and it was gone. It left me."

"To pursue a research fellowship?" the boy asked.

Gently the man placed his palm down on the counter. "Why naturally, son. A vagina does not vanish without a fellowship."

The café was quiet, the soft rain black and endless in the street outside. Wong took an epic pipe hit. "So you have been chasing the vagina for eleven years. You frazzled old rascal!"

For the first time, the man glanced at Wong. "Please don't be vulgar. Besides, I was not speaking to you." He turned back to the boy and said in a trusting and secretive undertone: "Let's not pay any attention to him. Okay?"

The paperboy nodded doubtfully.

"It was like this," the man continued. "I am a person who feels many things. All my life one thing after another has impressed me. Moonlight. Sausages. The hot chrome on a child-sized motorcycle. One thing after another. But the point is that when I had enjoyed anything there was a peculiar sensation as though it was laying around loose in me. Nothing seemed to finish itself up or fit in with the other things. Online support networks? I had my portion of them. The same. Afterwards laying around loose in me. I was a man who had never loved."

Very slowly he closed his eyelids, and the gesture was like a curtain drawn at the end of a scene in a play.

And then, suddenly, it was raining corpses. Actual human cadavers were falling from the sky in an irregular fashion. The paperboy could hear them thudding onto the concrete outside. Some were naked, but most were garbed in formal attire: business clothes and evening wear.

"Just try to ignore it, it's not important," said Wong.

The paperboy looked outside and saw that the slumped-over body of an accountant was partially blocking the entrance.

The man said: "The dissolution of the individual. A lake skirted with lilies, aimless in Spring. My own father falling like hail, but I can't experience his mind again."

Wong drew in his breath. "Time for wings, wings and wings. Nuclear fire sauce up the wazoo."

"Those sunless afternoons burying my face in the governess's skirts," said the man. "The ice age to end all ice ages."

"I smoke crack at work I don't give a fuck," Wong said. "Scoville units and NBA videos from the 90s all up in this bitch."

The paperboy was offered a plate of hot wings. He forced himself to ignore the scene outside, the steadily mounting mountain of dead. He lost himself in awareness of the fire sauce spreading through his mouth, obliterating his sensations in a soft blaze.

"Thousands of tiny pennies of heat amounting to a fortune of flavor," the paperboy said. "Mister, you've laid some wings on me and I'm partial to the burning Hell that lies on the other side of the conscious mind. A cauldron of furious lusts seething quietly with ghost peppers, scattering seeds of flame where it may. I wake in the night having soiled the sheets and wonder what is this voice that cries 'Come to the burning Hell!'"

Outside, fresh corpses were covering those that had already fallen.

"Not much to do but address the reality of climate change," the man said.

Wong bent down on one knee, as if he were about to propose.

"What are you doing?" the man asked.

"Genuflecting. One time I was about to take a piss and I heard someone mention impending global catastrophe and the probable end of the human race. Let me tell you that I was able to hold in my stream long enough to bend down for these terrible problems. A single tiny potato chip coated with the juice of a Carolina Reaper is about all I'm good for."

"Let's try a small test of that," the man said. " Why don't we stand in place and we'll see which one of us gets hit first."

"Just swell!" Wong sizzled. "I'm going to eat as much free-range bacon as I want to before I die so fuck all shit-hearted defeatist liberals. I've got a brand-new suit and I like to play Texas hold 'em when the mood hits. Time to max out on Scoville units!"

The paperboy made to stand, but before he could overturn the plate of wings, Wong had dashed out of the café. Moments later he was crushed by a falling corpse in a wedding dress.

"Ho ho ho, it's magic!" the man said.

TERMINAL BOWEL CANCER:
THE EQUANIMITY

Eric Nicholas had been married to Genevieve for forty-seven years and considered himself, now at seventy-two, to have lived a fulfilling and rich life with the partner of his choice and to have generally made the most of the various situations he had found himself in over the years. Life in Williamsport, Pennsylvania had proved adequately amenable to his admittedly modest ambitions and had granted him a number of friends and acquaintances of varying significance and long association.

On his way home from Walmart, where he had been laboring part-time after ostensibly retiring, Eric pulled his off-white 2006 Ford Taurus into the parking lot of the Lycoming Mall. Inside, he stopped at the restaurant known as "Friendly's" and ordered a grilled cheese sandwich and a Diet Sprite. Masticating the sandwich with his oral parts, he reflected on the numerous vicissitudes of his life that included the birth of his first son Dennis and the large amount of time spent in his garden tending to flowers such as zinnias and crocuses. And then there was the most significant—he would almost say critical—event of recent times, the event that was nothing other than his diagnosis with terminal bowel cancer.

Everything had been humming along agreeably in the twilight years of his life, until the weight loss and fatigue he had been experiencing for several months—and which he had struggled to dismiss as a side effect of his advancing age—progressed to abdominal pain and rectal bleeding. Temperamentally averse to visiting any kind of specialist, Eric did his best to ignore the situation until his wife confronted him one morning over their dual bowls of Kellogg's Special K Multigrain & Honey.

"Eric you are bleeding from the anus and you look like a ghost, please go see a doctor," Genevieve said. "I am your wife and I care about you greatly." Her eyes twinkled with spousal concern.

Uxoriously and yet reluctantly, Eric transported himself to the nearest proctologist. Rather than the mere gut inflammation and hemorrhoids he had been expecting, he was informed of his possession of metastatic colorectal cancer.

"Since the cancer has spread to the peritoneum and the tumor is right beside a main vein, palliative care is the best option at this point," Dr. Mussorgsky explained. "You could think of your intestines as winding Roman roads—once clean and reliable, but gradually taking on wear and tear over time. And this Stage IV terminal bowel cancer—it's a kind of colonic Vercingetorix. The invader is rude, unsophisticated and immensely vigorous. Unfortunately we can't simply take it out and strangle it, however satisfying that would be!"

Eric was summarily given six to eight months to live. Strangely, he quickly adjusted himself to his new, radically precarious existence. The gentle churchly faith of his ancestors had been like a small soft pillow on which the weary elbow of his awareness naturally came to rest when he fell onto the couch of contemplation. Now he used this pillow to smother the mewling kitten of death anxiety that was flexing its claws within him. A number of phone calls to Dennis and other family members were made, during which Eric generally maintained his equanimity, even as the revelation of incurable bowel cancer produced great weeping and consternation in his loved ones.

"Adjusting to life with terminal bowel cancer is a bit like learning to swim after being thrown in the deep end," Dr. Mussorgsky explained as they examined Eric's latest histology report. "I mean the deep end of the ocean with no one around, which means you're able to keep yourself afloat for a while by kicking and struggling and flailing, but eventually you run out of strength and sink into a frigid and anonymous grave. The situation with the basically incurable colorectal cancer is very similar. But the important thing is that you make the effort."

Eric perceived at once the truth of Dr. Mussorgsky's words and resolved to live out the time remaining to him with as much composure and dignity as he could manage. At times when he felt his inner strength fading, he reminded himself to enumerate the not inconsiderable blessings he had received over the course of his long life. He enumerated them in a tiny notebook he had bought at Dollar Tree and which he carried in the front pocket of his shirt. He examined the entries each night and usually added new ones derived from whatever memories had come to him during his periods of quiet reflection.

After finishing his sandwich and Sprite, Eric walked out of the Lycoming Mall and entered the parking lot, where he noticed that the path to his off-white 2006 Ford Taurus had been blocked by an elongated red van. FARM FRIENDS TRAVELING PETTING ZOO was stenciled on its side in large white letters, beneath which was a painting of several goggle-eyed horses, sheep and cows gamboling in a fenced-off enclosure. Small cages had been placed around the van, and each one was filled with animals, none of which corresponded to those in the painting; all Eric could see were puppies, rabbits, kittens and a white lamb with a black face and a missing right foreleg. A small crowd had formed around the cages, mostly parents with young children who were inspecting and in some cases stroking the rather dazed-looking animals.

Eric stopped in front of the van, not because he was interested in the animals, but because he wanted to watch the faces of the parents as they watched their children; in them he sensed something of the continuity of existence and the ongoing body of shared human experience larger than anyone's personal concerns. For a while he stood, considering profound matters of this nature; then he felt his mind returning to the reality of his impending death from an intestinal tumor.

A small boy was rubbing the head of the lamb with the missing foreleg. Eric decided to head over to the cage and examine the lamb for himself, and as he walked in its direction, he started to feel confused, then somehow silly. He felt that he had a terrible headache, and it seemed that it had been with him the entire day, although he knew this couldn't be possible. The distance to the cage appeared to increase the further he walked, and a numbness was settling over his left arm. He suddenly felt dizzy, and decided he would rest. He lowered himself to the ground.

Eric was dimly aware of a blaring siren, and of a great feeling of shuttling movement. People were talking to him, or moving around him, and various scenes were passing before his eyes with great rapidity. For a while he felt that he understood what was happening, but then the voices and the scenes lost all coherence. His body seemed to be moving through space even as he rested on his back. The people circling him were strangers, he was certain, and while he recognized emotions passing across their faces, it was impossible for him to determine what they were.

Finally he recognized Genevieve's presence, and with it he felt some of the logic of things return. He wanted to speak, to apologize for being late or otherwise inconveniencing her, but no words emerged.

Genevieve was explaining something about a spontaneous intracerebral hemorrhage, and Eric realized that he was now leaning back in a hospital bed. Some of the people around him appeared to be doctors, and some of them appeared to be the other sort of people who assisted doctors but were not doctors themselves, the word for which he could not recall.

In general Eric had great difficulty processing the situation, which was that the stroke had left him unable to readily speak or clearly think—a condition that would persist for the remainder of his existence, which was to conclude after four months instead of the expected six to eight.

"I didn't even consider that something like this could happen," Eric wanted to say. "I was too busy worrying about terminal bowel cancer!"

THE UNASSAILABLE VALUE
OF HUMAN DIGNITY

Pissing in my mouth; tearing off testicles; killing enemies; killing all enemies; amassing more territory; amassing more females; Spanish government granting me rights; killing children and crushing throats; amassing power; amassing food; amassing more females; warring with neighboring groups; crushing throats; amassing power; ethicist Peter Singer sympathizing with me; gaining territory; masturbating; pissing; shitting; masturbating;

Fearing others will take my place; killing their children; tearing out throats; amassing power; amassing food; pissing; shitting; humans approaching me; throwing shit at humans; running away from humans; screaming at humans; screaming; eating lower primates; biting off human fingers; Jane Goodall commenting on my lifestyle; crushing and eating children; satisfying my emotional needs at the expense of others; pissing in my mouth; amassing more females; masturbating;

Humans taking me out of my territory; humans putting me in artificial environments; humans making noises at me; humans giving me food; throwing shit at humans; amassing rocks to throw at humans; throwing rocks at humans;

Reading *Animal Liberation* by Peter Singer, realizing concept of 'rights' implies responsibilities; changing lifestyle to incorporate newly discovered concept of ethics; no longer killing children of enemy groups; no longer dismembering enemies; applying concepts of tolerance and liberalism to all aspects of life;

Applying for jobs in greater metropolitan area; showing up to job interviews wearing neatly-ironed suits; resisting urge to dismember job interviewer and smear shit across the walls; resisting urge to bite off human testicles;

Becoming concerned with environmental preservation; resisting urge to throw shit at humans; removing excess hair at salon; attempting to straighten posture; attending consciousness-raising seminars on interspecies cooperation;

Having sex with animal liberationist liberals and interspecies sex advocates; licking human vaginas; resisting urge to bite off human vaginal lips; experiencing insecurity over inch-long chimpanzee penis in comparison with longer human penises;

No longer feeling any attraction at all towards chimpanzee females; feeling like a tourist when attending human nightclub events; growing disenchanted with animal liberationists and interspecies sex advocates; attempting sex with mainstream human females;

Receiving condescending stares from unreconstructed humans when walking in public with human girlfriend; wondering whether human girlfriend genuinely cares about my emotional needs or is only interested in me as a chimpanzee; meeting human girlfriend's sincere liberal parents; feeling reassured by atmosphere of tolerance and inclusiveness;

Experiencing intense satisfaction from equal-partnership marriage; discussing emotional needs with human wife; dividing household chores equally with human wife; experiencing intense satisfaction from inclusive and liberal environments supportive of diversity; feeling reassured by the unassailable value of human dignity—

Wondering whether I have "sold out" and unreconstructed chimpanzees have more authenticity than me; feeling simultaneous jealousy and contempt when considering unreconstructed chimpanzees;

Instructing interspecies children not to bite off human testicles or smear shit on walls; instructing interspecies children not to smoke cigarettes; instructing interspecies children to avoid unreconstructed chimpanzees; encouraging interspecies children to pursue extracurricular activities;

Watching interspecies children smearing shit on walls; watching interspecies children biting off human testicles; watching interspecies children mating with unreconstructed chimpanzees; wondering why interspecies children regard me as outdated; discussing emotional insecurities with human wife;

Etc.

THE GRACE OF GOD

From a little after one o'clock until almost sundown of the hot dry dusty dead August afternoon, the Reprobate felt keenly the sense of something stalking him—that obscure impalpable dogged dauntless presence that he knew was nothing other than the divine grace he had dodged and dreaded his entire life.

John Francis Xavier O'Conor has written:

> *As the hound follows the hare, never ceasing in its running, ever drawing nearer in the chase, with unhurrying and imperturbed pace, so does God follow the fleeing soul by His Divine grace. And though in sin or in human love, away from God it seeks to hide itself, Divine grace follows after, unwearyingly follows ever after, till the soul feels its pressure forcing it to turn to Him alone in that never-ending pursuit.*

The Reprobate hoped he had a natural immunity to grace; that such an immunity could exist. But empirical evidence pointed to the distressing conclusion that no one, no matter his or her achievements in vice, was ever perfectly safe from the operation of grace. He recalled Old Ruprecht, an anticlerical indigent of his acquaintance who had lived for years as a cruel fatuous fanatical turpitudinous libertine of incomparable and almost undiscussable depravity. Selling children into slavery, deliberately folding laundry the wrong way, denying the Resurrection, urinating in public and other recreational activities had proceeded uninterrupted until the day when Old Ruprecht at last felt grace closing in. In desperation he had locked himself into the disabled toilet at Sam's Club and shouted sundry oaths to ward off God.

"Yahweh is a nefandous nincompoop," Old Ruprecht had fairly screamed. "The Resurrection is like the moon landing; it only happened in the imagination of sclerotic Irish landowners. The Holy Spirit is a wad of chewing gum stuck to the side of a toilet on a Greyhound bus."

At once the divine presence entered into his soul.

"Jesus was a chicken-hearted milksop," he protested. "The Sermon on the Mount is useless as livable advice."

But it was too late. C.S. Lewis has written:

> *That which I greatly feared had at last come upon me. In the Trinity Term of 1929 I gave in, and admitted that God was God, and knelt and prayed: perhaps, that night, the most dejected and reluctant convert in all England.*

However dejected and reluctant Lewis may have been, it is certain that Old Ruprecht surpassed him. He emerged from the Sam's Club toilet with his head bowed in bottomless remorse and took himself immediately to the St. Vincent de Paul Society, where he applied for work in a thrift store selling clothing and other donated items to the poor. When the Reprobate and his diversely scurrilous associates confronted him the next day, he looked frail and fouled with righteousness.

"I'd kill to smuggle some black market organs into Canada with you kids but instead I am giving away Hawaiian shirts to bums and now I'm helping out in a soup kitchen," Old Ruprecht had explained. "I mean I'd step over my own mother to feed a second-hand human liver to some street dogs in Montreal while slurping up bowl after bowl of Count Chocula and injecting cocaine into my penis, but studying the Scriptures and raising my sons to be men of God is about all I'm capable of now. I can't even litter."

The Reprobate suggested methamphetamine abuse, salutary alcoholism, underage prostitution and eating three entire boxes of Fig Newtons to relieve the grace, but nothing helped.

"I'd love to fire up the glass pipe and drink myself into incontinence after skull-fucking the shit out of some middle school hoes and dry-swallowing more Newtons than is strictly necessary for my daily caloric intake, but I'm too far sunk in redemption to even lift a finger. Grace of God ruined me, boys! I'm riding low on slave morality and hating every minute of it. Watch out for them torrents of shit-hot grace that will hit you when you least expect it."

The Reprobate and his allies departed in horror, certain that some new arrangement or device was necessary, some prophylactic against the operation of grace. Over the next few years they experimented with various prototypes, but only one showed any promise of resisting the inevitable. The Reprobate carried it with him now as he made his way down Main Street of the stagnant squalid sweltering town and approached the nearest Applebee's.

Evelyn Waugh has written:

> *I believe that everyone in his (or her) life has the moment when he is open to Divine Grace. It's there, of course, for the asking all the time, but human lives are so planned that usually there's a particular time—sometimes, like Hubert, on his deathbed—when all resistance is down and Grace can come flooding in.*

But now, for the Reprobate, grace was less flooding than seeping into his soul like acidulous droplets of urine from a busted septic tank in a cheap apartment on skid row. Jesus was a dung beetle rolling an immense ball of his discarded doubts and then pushing it, Sisyphus-like, up the hill of his conscience. He felt inclined to repent.

Shaking his head, the Reprobate decided to stab a man just to watch him die. He entered Applebee's and noticed several young professionals seated around a rectangular plate of chicken quesadillas. One of these suited types, a tow-headed unit with a Roman nose, was in the process of showing the others at the table a video on his Samsung Galaxy S9+. The Reprobate walked directly over to him, withdrew his Ka-Bar combat knife and buried it in the man's chest. The other men seated next to him were uncertain how to react to this unexpected stabbing and simply gaped like the fish that the Reprobate had caught in the creek as a child and held in the air to watch slowly expire.

"Now you is taken by sudden death," the Reprobate said. "No more power lunches and Excel spreadsheets for you, only imminent organ failure."

On Main Street again, several minutes later, the Reprobate kicked a homeless child in the teeth.

"Not just dental veneers but full-on implants to fix that, now. Hope you has reliable health coverage."

And then, as if it were deliberately emphasizing the distressing irrelevance of these maneuvers, the Reprobate felt a sudden convulsion of the soul, as if the soul had been seized by the need to defecate—the need to expel feces—when no toilet was near. Jesus was that obscure clenching in the bowels of the soul.

The Reprobate staggered into a Texaco Station and made for the freezer section. He had the shield with him, it was true, but he did not feel confident enough to use it just yet. He needed to buy time with one more sin of commission. After grabbing an Ice Cream Snickers bar, he headed for the counter, proceeding more slowly than usual. Several other customers got in line behind him, and when the Reprobate reached the counter he took a heavy change purse from his pocket.

"Just the ice cream? $1.50," said the clerk, a rabbit-faced teenager with an officious voice.

After pausing for dramatic emphasis, the Reprobate withdrew a series of pennies from the purse and slowly placed them on the counter, one on top of the other, until a small tower formed. He knew that God in his Heaven was incensed by sinners paying for ice cream bars with unnecessarily small change.

Another six minutes passed. The tower grew.

"Just break a fucking bill you prick," the clerk said.

The Reprobate responded with a stony glare and placed another penny down. The line of customers behind him grew, several of them voicing their impatience with miscellaneous profanity.

"Fucking shit there are like twenty people waiting can you not count out individual fucking coins?" the clerk said.

"These here pennies are legal U.S. tender and I will pay for this Ice Cream Snickers any way I like," the Reprobate said.

From some unidentifiable direction he sensed the hounds of God stalking him. The Divine Will was laying a trap for him, he knew, and it would take all his wits to escape it. He started another tower of coins.

"Jesus done thrown everything off balance," the Reprobate said. "Almost as if he was a panda bear that joined the cheerleader team. It wouldn't be right for that black and white bamboo-eating bear to publicly dance in a skirt. But that's what Jesus done gone did. The panda bear in the attic of my soul is doing his peppy dance and all I can do is watch. It ain't right that I have to watch that wild black and white bear doing his peppy dance and munching the slender green stalks."

"Jesus never existed UGGGHH JUST PAY WITH A NOTE OR A CARD FUUUUUUCK," the clerk said.

Several more minutes crawled by as the Reprobate assembled his tiny copper towers on the counter. Finally, he placed the last penny and raised his gaze to the clerk.

"WTF is this the shittiest challenge video ever or something, I mean is someone actually filming this?" asked the clerk. "Okay take your fucking Snickers asshole. Here's your receipt now fuck off forever."

"Stabbed a man just to watch him die," the Reprobate muttered.

"I don't care if you administered lethal injections to a busload of orphans, just get the fuck out of here okay NEXT PLEASE!"

The Reprobate departed, leaving the Snickers on the counter behind him. He could feel the grace of God scouring his soul, and knew at last that it was time for him to act.

Outside, as he felt Jesus wringing his heart like an old dish cloth, the Reprobate held the grace shield by the shaft and opened its nylon canopy to the sky, the eight sections forming a circle when seen from above, a black field on which had been embroidered, in bright scarlet letters:

☺ NON SERVIAM ☺

At once the Divine presence evacuated the area like oxygen sucked from a vacuum. All scrutiny ceased; the hounds of God fled.

There was no grace. There was no redemption. There was not even accountability.

If Hell is the absence of God, then the Reprobate was now alone in its deepest abyss—which seemed to be a place of vast relief and endless possibility. It was a place of cheap party hats and ready-to-eat chicken products, a place of unpaid taxes and double-parked cars. It was a place where he could have sex with farm animals on someone else's private property and know that, outside of flimsy legal constructs, there were no real consequences. Joy was general; doubt was absent.

The Reprobate returned home, his eyes lifted to the heavens in proud impiety, safe in the knowledge that God, though not in any sense dead, had never in his wisdom foreseen the construction of a sassily blasphemous umbrella.

DEUTSCHLAND '18

Karlheinz awoke refreshed and, after a light breakfast of Baumkuchen and Wurstsalat washed down with a Pilsner, resumed progress on the Gesamtkunstwerk. He was thinking of adding more toggle switches and a fuzzy rug to achieve the desired Verfremdungseffekt, but realized he had left these items back at his Arbeitsplatz. He would have to pick them up after his meeting with Charlotte.

Charlotte was a Hausfrau he had met at a Kaffee-klatsch in Düsseldorf. Her hobbies were reading Bildungsromans and playing the Katzenklavier. Karlheinz had bonded with her over their shared interest in solving the Welträtsel. Today they were going for a drive on the Autobahn followed by a trip to the Hamburger Kunsthalle to look at historical hamburgers.

Karlheinz fiddled with the Gesamtkunstwerk for a while longer, then smoked his Meerschaum. Sustained effort on the project usually left him with a feeling of Sehnsucht, and of late his Weltanschauung had been tainted with Weltschmerz.

Soon Charlotte arrived, accompanied by Günther, her pet Dachshund. Karlheinz hopped into her

Volkswagen and they were soon speeding along the Autobahn.

"Have you given any thought to moving into a new apartment? I don't know how you can fit that enormous Gesamtkunstwerk into such a tiny space," Charlotte said.

"No, no, I still have plenty of Lebensraum," Karlheinz replied. He popped a tape into the cassette deck, and soon they were listening to a mixture of popular tunes from Einstürzende Neubauten, Franz Schubert, Kraftwerk, Alec Empire, Richard Wagner, Nina Hagen and Carl Maria von Weber.

They stopped at a Kindergarten to pick up some Kinder Surprise. Charlotte's egg contained a miniature replica of the Bauhaus, while Karlheinz's contained a Poltergeist. From there, it was only a short trip to the Kunsthalle. As they were walking through the doors, they bumped into Karl Lagerfeldt.

"Well, hello, Karl," Charlotte said. "It's so nice to see you again. Of late with what have you been preoccupied?"

"I've spent the last six months in the Neandertal Valley with some Neandertals, studying a Lagerstätte," said Lagerfeldt. "By the way, would you care for a Lager?"

He handed her a foaming mug.

"Come along Charlotte, I'm interested in seeing what kind of Kitsch Hamburgers there are in this Kunsthalle," Karlheinz said.

"You'd better be quick," said Lagerfeldt. "According to Der Spiegel, the political situation is rapidly deteriorating. Now that Jakob Böhme and Ernst Jünger have joined the Baader-Meinhof Gang, the Molotov-

Ribbentrop Pact is in danger of being nullified. The Kaiser is ready to send in a Panzerdivision, and the Teutonic Knights have seized the Reichstag. It's turning into a regular Götterdämmerung."

Charlotte shook her hand in consternation. "Who does the Kaiser think he is, Caesar?"

Karlheinz and Charlotte proceeded inside the Kunsthalle. There were countless exhibitions of not only Hamburgers but also Frankfurters and Wienerschnitzel. Before long they bumped into Helmut Newton, who was photographing a particularly notable Knackwurst.

"Karlheinz?" Newton exclaimed. "I thought you were already here!"

"You must be mistaken, we've just arrived."

"Really? Then what are you doing over there?"

Karlheinz looked over and saw that he was indeed already present in the room, in the form of a Doppelgänger. The two of them regarded each other with antipathy.

"You'd best make yourself scarce," Karlheinz said. "I'm doing research for my Gesamtkunstwerk and I don't need you in the way."

"My Gesamtkunstwerk is better than your Gesamtkunstwerk!" said the Doppelgänger. "And my Weltschmerz is bigger than your Weltschmerz."

"This Doppelgänger is a bit of an Untermensch," Karlheinz thought. "I wonder how I can get rid of him?"

His thoughts were interrupted by Lagerfeldt, who had rushed into the room. "The Teutonic Knights are dispatching the Luftwaffe to exterminate the Lumpenproletariat!" he cried. "We've got to get out of here!"

Everyone rushed out of the Kunsthalle. Outside, they saw the Baader-Meinhof Gang climbing over the Berlin Wall. Karlheinz used his Poltergeist to knock them back, but there were too many to stop, and soon he and his friends were dodging bullets. Karlheinz grabbed his Doppelgänger and threw it into the line of fire. He felt a certain Schadenfreude as he watched it dying in his place.

Obersturmbannführer Martin Heidegger came into view atop the wall. "Our Rottweilers have taken Bayreuth by Blitzkrieg, and our Zeppelins are closing in on Cologne. Surrender now!" he cried.

Just then a Messerschmitt Me 262 piloted by Marlene Dietrich flew overhead. While the enemy was distracted, Karlheinz took out the Panzerfaust he always carried in his knapsack and fired it at the wall. Heidegger and the other members of the Baader-Meinhof Gang perished in the explosion.

"The Peace of Westphalia is saved!" exclaimed Lagerfeldt.

Everyone congratulated Karlheinz on his valor.

"What will you do now?" Helmut Newton asked.

"I might take a brief vacation in the Venus-berg," Karlheinz said. "But after that it's going to be Gesamtkunstwerk, Gesamtkunstwerk, Gesamtkunstwerk! I'm confident I can capture the Zeitgeist."

"With what will you capture it?" asked Charlotte.

"Perhaps with my handy Poltergeist. I just need a few more toggle switches and some fur."

Laughing, they all proceeded to a nearby Biergarten for some Strudel.

THE VAGUE AND TERRIBLE
UNCERTAINTY

Seeking refuge from the interminable hum of profit-less commerce that, like some ominous massing of spectral insects, penetrated every corner of the de-praved and decayed town, Grinderman found himself trudging along the path that led through the forest—somewhat thoughtlessly, as if his feet were carrying him along of their own accord, in revolt against the routine perambulations of his everyday existence. Around him, shrubberies, copses and other arboreal affairs conducted themselves in their usual swaying, mindless fashion, obeying the dictates of the wind and, perhaps, other, even less tangible masters.

Grinderman's botanical knowledge was scant, but he noted that, though it was still midsummer, a nearly indescribable autumnal atmosphere permeated the forest, lending the stolid trunks and wavering branch-es an attitude of forlorn resignation that made them seem perceptibly cognizant of their own incipient de-cay, held at bay by an almost conscious effort of leafy will. As he advanced deeper into a shaded canopy of what he took to be beech trees, but which could also perhaps have been elms, pines or maples—the precise distinction seemed curiously absent—he felt himself subsumed into an order of remoteness wholly separate from anything he had experienced. Another world seemed obscurely to be pressing upon him, and vague sensations of creeping unease besieged his senses, which themselves took on a heightened acuteness. The sound of each rustling leaf and crackling twig took on an exaggerated crispness, while the wind itself raised and lowered its pitch in what occurred to him as an almost intentional mockery of human intonation. The predominantly drab colors of bark and branch assumed a morbidly vibrant saturation, with lighter shades—the green of each sharply outlined leaf and the violent yellow of flowers underfoot—achieving an insistent and loathsome verdancy.

As he advanced further, Grinderman realized that he had lost his bearings and somehow strayed from what he had taken to be a well-defined and clearly recognizable path. Solitude had crept upon him like a thieving beggar and was now emptying the pockets of his certainty. He found himself surrounded by ancient tree trunks towering up like sentinels, and through a rent in the branches overhead he perceived the naked stars, which now seemed torn from their familiar constellations and rearranged in an unutterable chaos beyond any sane pictorial interpretation. This new lunatic arrangement infected him with dizziness, and he tore his gaze down again only to find his surroundings even less recognizable than they had seemed before. He was now thoroughly lost, and could no longer maintain any certainty of escape from this degenerate wilderness.

Night had comprehensively fallen, and as he stumbled blindly through the forest under the merciless scrutiny of the silent, staring stars, Grinderman seemed almost to be tumbling through illimitable and half-glimpsed abysses of obsidian darkness marbled with obscene and irrational nightmares, that were also black and dark. A vague and terrible uncertainty overcame him, one wholly beyond sane and objective analysis, that manifested to him as a storm of abstract nouns buffeting his consciousness: desolation, disquiet, damnation, derangement. Then, as if these nouns were, in fact, phantoms harrying and oppressing him, he perceived a series of adjectives afflicting them like astral parasites: amorphous, insensate, tremulous, febrile. These monstrous conjunctions of vague nouns with even vaguer adjectives plunged him further into some Tartarean purgatory of tenebrous inapprehensibility, a swirling vortex of nameless and malign mystery.

In desperation Grinderman fumbled in his pocket for his iPhone, and immediately called Dr. Selleck. The physician answered within moments, and at the sound of his voice Grinderman imagined Dr. Selleck seated in his office, visualizing in particular his bushy hair and enormous, outdated mustache.

"I'm in the forest," Grinderman muttered, as if this would explain everything.

"It's a nice day for that," said Dr. Selleck. "Enjoying the outdoors?"

"It's getting a bit cosmic," Grinderman choked out in a muffled voice. "Too much undefined portent. Feeling a bit ill."

"Probably related to intestinal distress," Dr. Selleck said. "I suggest eating something to fill the void . . . some kind of sandwich . . . ideally with meatballs. A Diet Coke would probably help too."

"Okay. I'm not sure I can actually get out of the forest."

"Just keep your head down and run at full speed while swiping through matches on Tinder. You'll be out of there in no time."

How Grinderman made his way out of the forest later seemed to him the greatest mystery of all, but at length he found himself emerging into a clearing. Along the way he had collided with a number of trees while running with his head down, and his body and clothes now bore an accumulation of lacerations. He did not recognize the narrow and insidiously snaking road before him either, and was forced to hail a taxi to make his way back to the depraved and decayed town of profitless commerce where he had subsisted for nearly the entirety of his unremarked existence.

As he stepped onto the nauseously familiar street that led to the main thoroughfare, Grinderman felt the ill-defined sensations that had afflicted him in the forest departing, replaced with a leaden impression of hopeless inertia that was perhaps equally unwelcome. Remembering Dr. Selleck's advice, he decided to avail himself of refreshment, but found that his usual haunts were now closed. Forced into perusing the poorly-lighted corners of back streets, Grinderman eventually located a collapsed-looking canteen whose sign advertised, through broken neon letters that made the words into the equivalent of a gap-toothed leer, an assortment of predictable victuals: burgers, kebabs, corn dogs, grinders. After pushing his way inside and drawing the attention of the man behind the counter—a mummified-looking geriatric in a shirt that had perhaps been white once but was now a stained beige, with a sharply-angled vermilion bow tie—he looked down at the menu and forced himself to concentrate.

At length, Grinderman ordered a grinder, along with a Diet Coke, as Dr. Selleck had suggested. He took a seat in the back; there were no other patrons, but he wanted to be as far away from the man at the counter as possible while he ate.

Grinderman inspected his tray, which was reassuringly square and solid-seeming. The can of Diet Coke with which he had been furnished appeared can-shaped and Coke-like, and did not connote any impression of elusive or illusory expectancy. The world seemed at last to have resumed its familiar contours.

Taking the grinder from its paper sleeve, he remembered that, on his few excursions to other towns—all of them undertaken in service of the Company, which had been his sole employer since the time he had left school—he had heard sandwiches of its kind referred to as subs, hoagies and even torpedoes.

"The only grinders we have are fish grinders," the man with the vermilion bow tie had told him when he had placed his order, and Grinderman now realized that this was true. Situated between two rounded slabs of bread was a thick wedge of battered fish garbed in a limp leaf of lettuce. Grinderman raised it to his mouth and was about to bite down when a stray thought stopped him. Was it in fact a grinder after all, or was it a sub, hoagie or torpedo? For a moment the uncertainty that had gripped him in the forest returned with the full efflorescence of its malevolence and, unmoored again, Grinderman felt his head swimming as if with a sudden and unexpected inebriation.

Struggling to regain his certainty, Grinderman dropped the sandwich onto the tray and pushed it away from him. The can of Diet Coke reared up at him like some Palaeogean obelisk of supremely doubtful provenance. He felt himself tormented again by adjectives and nouns that seemed to pertain to some order of gnostic immanence impervious to mere human cogitation. Worse, the sandwich now intersected with his personal reality in a previously unimagined, in fact undreamt of and, at all prior stages of his existence, thoroughly inconceivable manner. He felt himself reduced to a puppet of nameless ambient forces, jerked about fitfully in tremulous spasms of jittering agitation. The sandwich seemed to rear towards him at great speed, until he lost his balance and fell off his chair.

Closing his eyes, Grinderman felt himself tottering and yawing above the abyss again, and knew that if he did not act now, he would be lost forever. Blind and deaf, he groped above him for the sandwich and thrust it into his mouth. Chewing like a ravenous animal, he washed it down with enormous gulps from the can, spilling half of it in the process. Regaining his sanity was like groping for a glittering grain whilst swimming through twilit seas of primordial sludge, but at last he felt sustenance coursing through him, and the fog fell away.

Standing up, Grinderman felt the world solidify around him again. He wiped himself off with a handful of napkins and exited the canteen, eager to be away from the beige-shirted man with the vermilion bow tie who had witnessed the spectacle of his uncertainty with an attitude at once both sardonic and contemptuous.

Outside, Grinderman swore to himself that he would resume work at the Company with a new lightness of spirit, and he resolved never to observe nature again. As he departed into the night, he tossed the empty can of Diet Coke into an alleyway, and his tongue reached unconsciously to the corner of his lip to remove a trace of tartar sauce from the formerly Tartarean sandwich.

IF YOU'VE ENJOYED THIS BOOK,
WE KNOW YOU WILL FIND

PLEASANT TALES

BY BRENDAN CONNELL
STIMULATING
AND PULSE-QUICKENING
AS WELL.

IT IS PUBLISHED BY EIBONVALE
PRESS, AND COMES IN SEVERAL
EASY TO HANDLE FORMATS
FOR YOUR CONVENIENCE.

IF YOU WANT TO GET RID OF
HUMDRUM FEELINGS, PLEASE

SEEK IT OUT!

A PARTIAL LIST OF SNUGGLY BOOKS

CPSIA information can be obtained
at www.ICGtesting.com
Printed in the USA
FSHW01n1300240618
49580FS